Written by
Marc G. Daniels

DADERINA SERIES™

THE STORY OF DADERINA™

illustrated by
Azulita Studio

First paperback edition August 2021

For information contact us at **www.daderina.com**

Written by Marc G. Daniels
Illustrated by Azulita Studio

Acknowledgements
Special thank you to my wife, mom, aunt Larita and sister Felicia for your feedback in making this vision turn into a reality.

978-0-947482-20-6 (hardback)
978-0-947482-21-3 (paperback)
978-0-947482-22-0 (eBook)

Self Published

"This book is dedicated to my loving wife, Kim; and my three daughters: Giada, Isabella and Suri." - **MGD**

It was a late afternoon in May on the beautiful island of **Bermuda**. Sisters, Giada, Bella and Suri were in their car seats singing and playing. Mommy and Daddy were driving the two older girls to the first dress rehearsal for their ballet performance at the Earl Cameron Theatre.

Giada, the eldest, asked her parents,
"Can we buy some ice cream?"
Bella, the middle sister, shouted, "Yes! Me too,
pleeeeeeease?"

Baby Suri giggled, "Hee hee" and waved her hands in delight. Daddy told the girls that he would buy them all ice cream **after** they had danced on stage.

The girls were super excited! The older two sisters could not wait to get on stage. Oh, how they loved to jump and twirl!

When they arrived at the Theatre, Daddy told the girls how much he loved them. "Don't forget to smile and have fun! You will be amazing!"

Mommy took Giada and Bella by their little hands and held them tightly as they entered through the Theatre doors to join the rest of their class.

"It's time to dance" said Mommy, as they ascended the grand staircase into the Theatre.

8

Once inside, Giada and Bella sat down with their classmates.

The little ballerinas were enchanted by the older dancers as they watched them prepare to go on stage.

Bella relished this moment! She was desperate to hit the stage with her big sister and show everyone how well she had practiced her moves. However, she was still learning to be patient. Bella showed great composure despite being the youngest in the class; but it was not easy and her mind started to wander.

Meanwhile, Daddy waited in the lobby with baby Suri who had fallen asleep, snuggled in his arms.

11

Back in the Theatre, Giada and Bella had been waiting a long, LONG, LONGGGG time for their turn to take to the stage.

By now, Bella had lost interest in dancing. Instead, she wanted her Daddy to come hug her and take her to the ice cream parlor.

Mommy tried to encourage Bella to remain patient, "It will just be a little bit longer my love."

Bella did not want to wait another minute! She began shouting, "I WANT MY DADDY; I want my Daddy NOW!"

The ballet teacher became worried.

"What should I do?" she wondered. "I know", she thought to herself. "I will go and find her Daddy right now. That will cheer Bella up!"

The teacher huffed and puffed as she hurriedly ran to find Daddy in the lobby. "There he is. Wait, is he sleeping on the sofa?" Yes, Daddy had fallen asleep with baby Suri!

"Wake up!" she said. "Bella needs you, right now!"

14

15

Daddy **jumped** to his feet. Startled, he rushed backstage with baby Suri bouncing in his arms.

Once there, Daddy could see Bella crying on Mommy's lap.

"What's the matter, Bella?" asked Daddy.

Bella answered, "Daddy, I don't think ...."

Before Bella could express how she was feeling, another ballet teacher yelled out, "Up next, Pre-Ballet. Get ready girls. Go go go!"

"Come on my little love." Daddy said happily. "It's your turn to dance."

Bella gave Daddy a nod of agreement. Daddy held Bella's hand while still holding baby Suri. Mommy took Giada by her hand and they escorted the girls to the side of the stage.

"Go ahead girls. Remember, you are bright shining stars," said Daddy.

Bella was the first to walk on stage, but she kept looking back, with her eyes fixed on her Daddy, as she stepped further and further away from him.

"Noooooooo!" she screamed. "I want my Daddy!"

Then, Bella flopped to the ground. "No, no, NOOOOOOOO!!!" yelled Bella, as she shook her head back and forth.

Giada tried to grab Bella's little hand to comfort her but at that moment, Bella only wanted her Daddy.

Daddy knew just how much Bella wanted to dance. And so, Daddy's mind started to race. "How can I help Bella find her **confidence** and **joy**?"

So, what did Daddy do? While holding baby Suri, Daddy ran onto the stage and stood right next to Bella. When Giada saw Daddy, she smiled. "Look Bella, **Daddy is here**!"

Daddy asked Bella, "Would you like to dance with me?"

Bella nodded in agreement.

Without hesitation, Daddy found his rhythm and began to **dance**!

Daddy knew all the moves because Daddy always watched Giada and Bella practice at home.

Bella immediately felt happy. With a grin, she began to twirl.

As Daddy held baby Suri, he did a Pirouette followed by a Temps Leve Arabesque and then a flying Pas de Chat, a few of the most loved ballet moves.

Giada was impressed. Bella could not stop smiling.

"Daddy is really, really, REALLY GOOD," said Giada.

Bella started to follow her Daddy, first with a Pirouette to the left and then a Pirouette to the right.

Bella felt confident, so much so that she forgot all about her ice cream – at least for the moment.

27

Next, Daddy held Bella's hand. Bella took hold of Giada's hand. Giada then held another student's hand until they all made a circle. First, they tip-toed inward making a small circle then they tip-toed outward making an even bigger circle. This was not part of the original routine, but Daddy was making the whole class giggle.

Then each of the ballerinas took their final bow.

When the music ended, Bella did not want to stop dancing. She was now ready for the main event to begin to showcase her talent.

Daddy's eyes filled with tears that sparkled from the bright stage lights.

Bella led the way off stage and walked straight into Mommy's loving arms. Bella whispered to Mommy, "Daddy is the best dad. He is a really good ballerina! He is the best DADerina in the whole world!"

"He's a super Daderina!"

"This made my heart so happy."

"This made me cry with joy."

"What a great father!"

"She needed the support and he was there. How wonderful that she can feel so safe and secure."

One week later, Giada and Bella were on stage for their actual performance. Bella danced with confidence, smiled and took a bow.

The End

About the Author

Marc G. Daniels is a lawyer from Bermuda of Italian and African ancestry. In 2018, Entertainment Tonight voted Marc the 'Father of the Year'.

instagram @DaderinaBermuda
www.daderina.com

photo courtesy of Amanda Temple

About the Book

The Story of Daderina™ documents a spontaneous demonstration of love, caught on camera, shared on social media, which became a global sensation.

About the Series

Daderina™ is an emotional & witty series that captures the essence of parenting, childhood, love and laughter. The series is designed to encourage and highlight the strength of fathers who unselfishly give their time and energy to uplift their offspring,even if it means stepping out of their comfort zone.

About the Azulita Studio

Azulita Studio Azulita Studio is a creative studio based in Florianópolis, Brazil. Created by the partnership and longtime friendship between the illustrators Camilla Souza and Milla Bioni.
It was born with the intention of bringing together the experiences and skills of these artists.

Working as a team they are able to create images that delight and thrill in a higher quality.
The studio specializes in creating illustrations for children's books, editorials, booklets and character design.
Both graduated in Visual Arts, they have been working with illustration since 2014.

Instagram @azulita.studio
www.azulitastudio.com